It Wasn't My Fault

It Wasn't My Fault

Helen Lester

Illustrated by Lynn Munsinger

SCHOLASTIC INC.
New York   Toronto   London   Auckland   Sydney

ISBN 0-590-48645-4

12 11 10 9 8 7 6   5 6 7 8 9/9

Printed in the U.S.A.   09

First Scholastic printing, July 1994

Things did not always go well for Murdley Gurdson.

He couldn't control the toothpaste.
He fell into wastebaskets.

And he dropped only valuable vases.
Whatever happened, it was usually his fault.

One day he went for a walk
in his one too big new shoe.
He had stepped out of the other one.
He couldn't remember where.

Before long someone laid an egg on
Murdley Gurdson's head.

He looked at a nearby bird.
"Did you lay an egg on my head?" he asked.

"I did," confessed the bird, "but it wasn't my fault. A horrible aardvark screamed and scared me."

So Murdley Gurdson and the bird went to
see the aardvark.

"Did you scream and scare the bird into laying
an egg on Murdley Gurdson's head?" they asked.
"I did," confessed the aardvark.
"But it wasn't my fault."

"A nasty, pygmy hippo stepped on
my tail and a scream just popped out."

Together they went to find the pygmy hippo.
"Did you step on the aardvark's tail, making him
scream and scare the bird into laying an egg
on Murdley Gurdson's head?" they asked.

"I did," confessed the pygmy hippo.
"But it wasn't my fault.
I did it by accident when I was getting
out of the way of a hopping shoe with long ears."
"A WHAT?" they all asked.

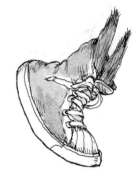

Just then along came a hopping shoe
with long ears.

With a pull and a tug, they soon found that the ears were attached to a rabbit.

"It wasn't my fault," the rabbit explained.

"I was hopping along when I landed in that shoe and became stuck."

The shoe looked very much like the new too big
shoe Murdley had stepped out of some time ago.

In fact, it was.

Murdley thought:
"The rabbit became stuck in my shoe and frightened
the pygmy hippo who stepped on the aardvark's tail.
The aardvark screamed and scared the bird into
laying an egg on my head."

"Then I suppose it was *my* fault," Murdley Gurdson said very sadly.
Two tears splashed on his new too big shoes.

"There, there," said the pygmy hippo, the rabbit,
the bird, and the aardvark, "don't cry."
"It was my fault," said the bird.
"It was my fault," said the aardvark.
"It was my fault," said the pygmy hippo.
"I think it was the shoe," said the rabbit.
"Let's go back to your house and do something
about that egg."

They all went into the kitchen.
The aardvark turned Murdley Gurdson upside
down and the egg plopped into a pan.
The rabbit ground the pepper.
The pygmy hippo added a pinch of salt.
The bird ran around and around in the pan
doing a very fine job of scrambling.

Murdley Gurdson enjoyed every bite of his
scrambled egg.

Murdley thanked his friends.
He went to the door to let them out
and . . .

. . . . it wasn't his fault!